Text Copyright © Cao Wenxuan

Illustration Copyright © Qin Xiuping

Edited by Denice Jasper

English Copyright © 2018 by Cardinal Media, LLC.

ISBN 978-1-64074-006-8

Through Phoenix Juvenile and Children's Publishing Ltd.

Printed in China

2 4 6 8 10 9 7 5 3 1

The Call of the Sky

Written by **Cao Wenxuan** • Illustrated by **Qin Xiuping**

One day a young farmer's boy found an egg that looked like the goose eggs at his father's farm. He brought it home and carefully put it underneath the mother goose, who was just starting to lay her own eggs. "One more baby goose. Isn't that nice?" he thought.

After some time, the eggs began to hatch. One by one, the baby geese pecked their way out of their shells. It wasn't until that evening that the last egg, the one the boy had found, hatched. This little baby had two black spots, one above each eye. His family called him Spot.

Since farm geese can't fly, the mother goose taught her babies to swim. All summer, they played and swam in the water.

One day, a dragonfly flew past, catching Spot's attention.

The dragonfly disappeared into the reeds. But a dog had
quietly followed Spot and waited until Spot had wandered
far away from his mother and all his brothers and sisters.
The dog rushed out of the reeds and pounced!

Squawk! Squawk! Spot shouted.

Spot's mother and the rest of his family
came to save him! They attacked the dog
without worrying about their own safety.

Spot was grateful to his family. *Krronk! Krronk!* His mother
and all his brothers and sisters called out happily.

By autumn, the little geese had grown almost as big as their mother. Spot's family thought he was the best-looking goose ever.

In winter, the flock opened their wings and flapped at the snow. They were a very happy family.

Spring arrived. Spot and his family were eating grass by the
river when they heard wonderful sounds coming from the sky.

Honk! Honk! A wedge of swans filled the sky.

Spot was amazed. He'd never seen anything fly so beautifully.

Honk! The lead swan cried out once more.
It sounded like a clear trumpet call to Spot.

When the swans had
almost disappeared into
the distance, Spot began
to flap his wings.
Suddenly, with a big
whoosh, he launched
himself into the air.

The mother goose and all his brothers and sisters couldn't believe their eyes.

Krronk! Krronk! Krr-onk! They called to the sky.

As evening tinged the sky with red,
a black dot appeared in the sky.
The dot drew closer and closer.
It was a swan. It was Spot!

Spot flew in a circle and landed
gracefully.

The mother goose and all his
siblings gathered around him,
beating their wings in joy.

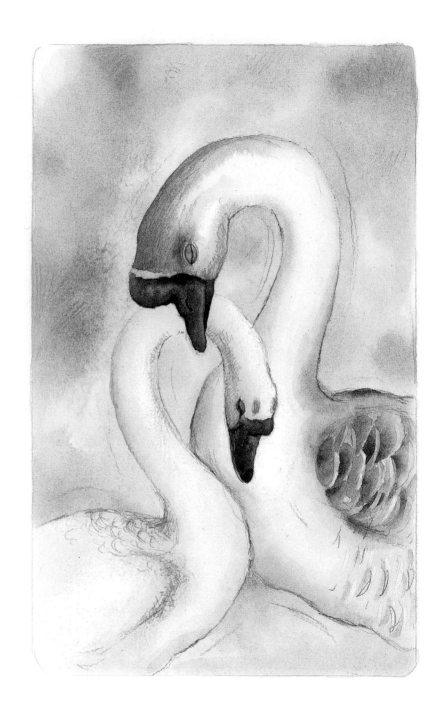

The days that followed seemed uneventful, and Spot would often look up to the sky.

The mother goose spent more time with Spot.

Autumn came and the world turned
from green to gold. Spot began to
feel uneasy. He was looking forward
to hearing that sound in the sky, but
was afraid to hear it too.

Finally, the sound echoed throughout the sky. *Honk! Honk!*

The mother goose and all her children quickly looked up. But Spot kept his head down and ate the last patch of green grass.

The swans flew past and circled in the sky above. Spot unfurled his wings, but not to fly. He hid his head underneath them, as if it was a quiet night and he had gone to sleep.

Honk! Honk! All the swans were calling out,
and their trumpeting filled the sky.

As the swans flew off, the honking began to fade. Spot slowly lifted his head from under his wings. He craned his neck high and heard the last call trailing off. *Honk...*

Spot slowly opened his wings, but then he folded them back. He opened them once more, then folded them back again. Finally, with a *whoosh*, he flapped his wings and launched himself into the sky.

He didn't fly away, but flew in circles above the farm, above his mother, above his brothers and sisters.

When Spot saw the swans had almost disappeared over the horizon, he heard his mother's voice. "Go, child. If you don't go now you'll miss your chance." Then all his family called, "Go Spot! We'll be waiting for you here next spring."

He looked down at his family one last time.

Honk! His call filled the sky.

He set off, flying into the distance, toward the horizon.